To.

David & Jennifer.

Merry Christmas.

Stories re-told by Anne McKie, illustrations by Ken McKie.

This edition published 1992.

Published by
Grandreams Limited
Jadwin House, 205/211 Kentish Town Road, London, NW5 2JU.

Printed in Czechoslovakia.

ISBN 0 86227 905 4

LO3

My Best Book of FAIRY TALES & Nursery Rhymes

Contents

Red Riding Hood

Aladdin

Sleeping Beauty

The Gingerbread Man

plus a selection of your favourite
Nursery Rhymes

This book belongs to
....
....
....
Age ....

SNOW WHITE

Once upon a time a lovely little Princess was born. She had hair as black as coal and skin as white as snow. "I know," smiled the Queen, as she gazed at her baby. "I shall call her Snow White!"

But soon after the little Princess was born, the Queen died, leaving the King very unhappy and lonely.

After some years had passed — and Snow White had grown up into a young lady — the King married again. His new Queen was very beautiful and also very vain.

On the wall of her room, the new Queen kept a magic mirror.

Because she couldn't bear to know of anyone more beautiful than herself, the Queen would look in her mirror every day and say, "Magic Mirror on the wall, who is the fairest one of all?" And the mirror would answer, "You are the fairest one of all!"

Now one dreadful day when the Queen asked her mirror the usual question, the mirror replied. "Snow White is the fairest one of all!"

The Queen was so angry and jealous she almost smashed the mirror.

As the Queen stood glowering into the mirror, she thought of a plan. She sent for her huntsman and ordered him to kill Snow White. The huntsman wished he had not been chosen to do such a dreadful thing, but he dare not disobey the wicked Queen.

He lifted Snow White onto his horse and rode with her deeper and deeper into the forest.

At last they stopped and Snow White begged him to spare her life.

The huntsman was far too kind to kill the beautiful Princess. Instead he rode quickly away — leaving Snow White in the care of the animals who roamed the forest.

Snow White spent all the day wandering through the trees. At first she felt frightened, but one by one the animals came out from their hiding places and made friends.

The time passed very quickly and soon it began to get dark. Some of the birds and animals seemed to be leading Snow White along a special path, so she followed them.

The forest path led to the strangest little house Snow White had ever seen. And finding no-one at home, she opened the door and walked right in.

Everything inside the house was very small. The ceiling was so low, that Snow White had to bend her head to walk about. ''Whoever lives here must be very tiny!'' laughed Snow White, as she picked up the dainty cups and bowls.

''There seems to be seven of everything,'' she gasped, as she looked round the room. ''Seven chairs to sit on, seven pipes to smoke and seven pairs of slippers.''

Now this was the home of the seven dwarfs who worked all day in the mountains digging for gold.

Snow White felt so tired she went upstairs to the bedroom, where she found seven little beds all in a row. She laid across three of them and fell fast asleep.

And that is how the dwarfs found her when they returned late that night. They agreed not to wake her, but let her sleep until morning.

The seven dwarfs had so many questions to ask Snow White. She told them about the wicked Queen and how she had tried to kill her. "Stay with us," begged the dwarfs. "The Queen will never find you here, for our house is deep in the forest."

So Snow White stayed. She cooked and cleaned and kept the tiny house tidy. And she promised the seven little men that she would never open the door to anyone when they were at work.

Meanwhile, back at the palace, the evil Queen stood in front of her magic mirror again. "Magic Mirror on the wall, who is the fairest one of all?" And the mirror answered, "Snow White is the fairest of them all!"

The Queen almost smashed the mirror in her rage. "Where is Snow White?" she screamed. And the mirror replied, "At the cottage of the seven dwarfs deep in the forest."

Quickly the wicked Queen disguised herself as an old woman. Next she filled a big basket full of apples. Then she chose the biggest, rosiest apple — and with the help of magic spells and potions — made the apple poisonous.

Feeling very pleased with herself she set off for the home of the seven dwarfs.

"How very lucky!" sniggered the Queen. For there was Snow White drawing water from the well outside the little house.

The old woman startled Snow White, and she fled inside and bolted the door. ''Don't be afraid of an old woman,'' cried the wicked Queen. ''All I ask is a drink of water from your well, and I will give you my rosiest apple in return.''

Snow White foolishly opened the window and held out her hand. The wicked Queen smiled. As soon as Snow White took one bite of the poisoned apple — she fell to the ground dead!

No sooner had the Queen returned to the Palace, than she pulled off her disguise and stood in front of her magic mirror. "You are the fairest of them all," the mirror told her. "Then Snow White is dead at last," smiled the Queen.

When the dwarfs returned from work, they guessed what had happened. Weeping with sorrow, they built a glass coffin for their beloved Snow White.

They placed it in a forest clearing and watched over her day and night.

One day a Prince was riding through the forest. When he saw the dwarfs looking so sad, he got off his horse to see what was the matter.

He listened to their sad tale, and as he gazed down at Snow White he fell in love with her at once.

As he bent down to kiss her, she opened her eyes and sat up. The spell was broken. The Prince helped her out of the glass coffin and all the dwarfs ran to hug her.

The Prince asked Snow White to marry him and she gladly agreed.

The next time the wicked Queen stood in front of her Magic Mirror, it said to her, "Snow White is the fairest of them all!" That made her fall into such a jealous rage, that she fell down dead.

So the story ends happily after all, for the Prince, Snow White and the seven dwarfs — but not for the wicked Queen of course!

Lavender's blue, dilly, dilly,
Lavender's green,
When I am king, dilly, dilly,
You shall be queen.

Jack Sprat could eat no fat,
His wife could eat no lean,
And so between them both, you see,
They licked the platter clean.

Six little mice sat down to spin;
Pussy passed by and she peeped in.
What are you doing, my little men?
Weaving coats for gentlemen.
Shall I come in and cut off your threads?
No, no, Mistress Pussy, you'd bite off our heads.
Oh, no, I'll not; I'll help you to spin.
That may be so, but you don't come in.

Cock a doodle doo!
My dame has lost her shoe,
My master's lost his fiddling stick
And knows not what to do.

Cock a doodle doo!
What is my dame to do?
Till master finds his fiddling stick
She'll dance without her shoe.

Tom, Tom, the piper's son,
Stole a pig and away did run;
The pig was eat,
And Tom was beat,
And Tom went howling
Down the street.

Roses are red,
Violets are blue,
Sugar is sweet
And so are you.

There was an old woman
Lived under a hill,
And if she's not gone
She lives there still.

Punch and Judy
Fought for a pie;
Punch gave Judy
A knock in the eye.

Says Punch to Judy,
'Will you have any more?'
Says Judy to Punch,
'My eye is too sore.'

Hickety, pickety, my black hen,
She lays eggs for gentlemen;
Sometimes nine, and sometimes ten,
Hickety, pickety, my black hen.

The north wind doth blow,
And we shall have snow,
And what will poor Robin do then,
Poor thing?
He'll sit in a barn,
And keep himself warm,
And hide his head under his wing,
Poor thing.

Monday's child is fair of face,
Tuesday's child is full of grace,
Wednesday's child is full of woe,
Thursday's child has far to go,
Friday's child is loving and giving,
Saturday's child works hard for its living,
And the child that's born on the Sabbath day
Is bonny and blithe, and good and gay.

Thursday

Little Tommy Tucker
  Sings for his supper,
What shall we give him?
  White bread and butter.
How shall he cut it
  Without e'er a knife?
How shall he marry
  Without e'er a wife?

Lucy Locket lost her pocket,
  Kitty Fisher found it;
Not a penny was there in it,
  Only ribbon round it.

The Lion and the Unicorn
were fighting for the crown,
The Lion beat the Unicorn
all round the town.
Some gave them white bread
and some gave them brown,
And some gave them plum cake,
and drummed them out of town.

Red sky at night,
Shepherd's delight;
Red sky in the morning,
Shepherd's warning.

PINOCCHIO

This story took place when all toys were made of wood, and this tale is one of the strangest ever told.

Can you believe that an ordinary log of wood could become a real live boy? Read on and you will see.

One day a carpenter picked up a log of wood from a pile in the corner of his workshop. He was just about to chop it with his axe when he heard a little voice cry, "Don't hurt me!" The voice came from the log of wood.

The carpenter was so terrified that he opened the door and was about to throw the log away, when who should come by but Geppetto the toymaker. "Just what I need," cried the old man. "I am going to carve a puppet that will behave just like a real boy."

The carpenter was pleased to get rid of the talking log, because he thought it was bewitched!

Back at his toy shop Geppetto started work straight away. First he carved the puppet's head, and an amazing thing happened . . . the eyes blinked and the mouth smiled. Next he carved the body right down to the toes.

All of a sudden the puppet's foot flew up and kicked the old man on the nose. Instead of being angry, Geppetto was delighted with his talking puppet. "I shall call you Pinocchio," he smiled, "and you shall call me Father."

Geppetto began to teach Pinocchio how to walk. No sooner had the puppet learned, than he dashed out of the door and ran off down the street. Suddenly, a large policeman stepped out in front of Pinocchio and grabbed him.

By now a crowd had gathered and Geppetto was shouting at Pinocchio for running away. The angry crowd told the policeman to lock the old man up, for he was being cruel to the puppet.

So the policeman took poor Geppetto away to prison and Pinocchio ran off home.

You will have guessed by now that Pinocchio had a mind of his own, and was going to do exactly as he liked!

Later on Geppetto was let out of prison, because he had done nothing wrong. He made Pinocchio promise that he would go to school and learn to read.

That night Geppetto made him some new clothes. "All I need now, father, is a spelling book," said Pinocchio. "Then I shall be like other boys."

At once the kind old man went out into the cold night and sold his only coat, to buy the spelling book.

Next morning, Pinocchio set off to school. But what was that wonderful sound he could hear? It was the music of a fairground.

He forgot all about school when he spotted a "Puppet Theatre". Without a second thought Pinocchio sold his spelling book to buy a ticket to go inside.

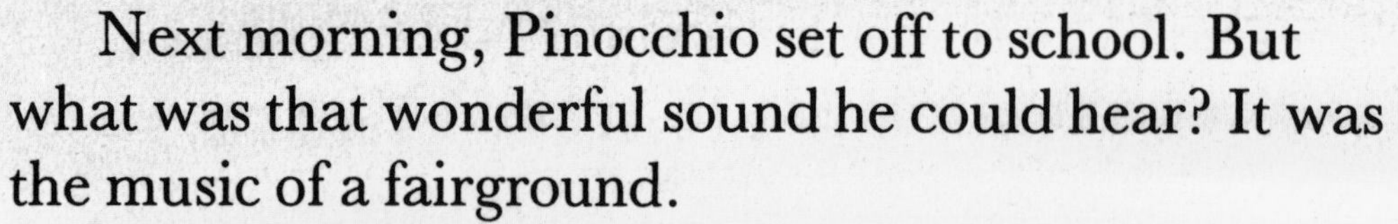

But when the puppets saw Pinocchio, they shouted for him to come up on stage to join them. The whole performance was ruined! The puppet-master threatened to throw Pinocchio on the fire — like a log of wood.

However, Pinocchio cried so pitifully that the puppet-master gave him five pieces of gold to take to Geppetto.

On his way home, Pinocchio met a sly fox and a cat who pretended to be blind. They told the puppet that if he buried his gold in a certain field — a miracle would happen. A tree would grow ladened with gold pieces.

It was a trick, of course! And when Pinocchio returned the next day the five gold pieces had gone, and so had the fox and the cat.

Not content with stealing his money, the fox and cat disguised themselves as robbers. They grabbed Pinocchio and tried to hang him from a tree, then ran off leaving him to die.

Luckily for Pinocchio, the Blue Fairy lived nearby and she saved him. She sent her poodle-dog footman to fetch the doctors . . . and what strange doctors they turned out to be . . . a crow, an owl and a cricket.

They all decided that Pinocchio was not dead after all — he was just a wicked puppet that had run away.

The Blue Fairy asked Pinocchio to tell.her about his adventures, but the puppet would not tell the truth. The more he lied, the longer his nose grew. It grew so long it stuck out of the window.

The Blue Fairy clapped her hands and several birds flew down and they pecked at Pinocchio's nose until it was the right size once more.

"That's what comes of telling lies!" laughed the Blue Fairy.

"How can I become a real boy?" Pinocchio asked the Blue Fairy.

"If you are good and go to school, you will have your dearest wish," she promised.

So Pinocchio went back to school. He worked hard, but unfortunately he soon grew tired of being good. He made friends with the naughtiest boy in the class.

One night they decided to run away to Toyland (where there is no school). They climbed into a special coach pulled by donkeys, and off they went.

It seemed fun at first, no lessons or work for months. Pinocchio and his friend loved it.

Then, without any warning, Pinocchio woke up to find he had grown a pair of donkey's ears. His friend had already changed into a donkey. All the children who came to Toyland were changed into donkeys, too, then sold.

A circus ringmaster bought poor Pinocchio and worked him very hard. One day, when he was jumping through a hoop, he hurt his leg.

The circus didn't want a lame donkey, so Pinocchio was sold again. This time to a man who wanted to make the donkey's skin into a drum.

He dragged Pinocchio into the sea to drown him, but the puppet slipped out of the skin and swam away laughing.

Suddenly a great shark rose up from the waves. Its monstrous jaws opened up wide and swallowed Pinocchio in one bite.

Down and down went the puppet — right to the bottom of the shark's stomach. He felt very frightened, until he heard a voice he knew.

There was old Geppetto sitting in a boat, carving toys from the fish bone lying around.

Geppetto explained that he had gone to sea to look for Pinocchio and had been swallowed by the shark. He had lived on the food he had packed in his boat.

With the help of the Blue Fairy, the two sailed out of the shark's mouth and arrived safely back home.

Pinocchio sat down with Geppetto and told him all his adventures. He promised never to leave the old man again. And this time he kept his promise.

During the night, when Pinocchio was asleep, the Blue Fairy came by and granted Pinocchio his wish.

When he woke the next morning, he had become a real boy at last!

Old Mother Hubbard
Went to her cupboard,
To fetch her poor dog a bone;
But when she got there
The cupboard was bare
And so the poor dog had none.

She went to the baker's
To buy him some bread;
But when she came back
The poor dog was dead.

She went to the joiner's
To buy him a coffin.
But when she came back
The poor dog was laughing.

She took a clean dish
To get him some tripe;
But when she came back
He was smoking a pipe.

She went to the fishmonger's
To buy him some fish;
But when she came back
He was licking the dish.

She went to the tavern
For white wine and red;
But when she came back
The dog stood on his head.

She went to the fruiterer's
To buy him some fruit;
But when she came back
He was playing the flute.

She went to the tailor's
To buy him a coat;
But when she came back
He was riding a goat.

She went to the hatter's
To buy him a hat;
But when she came back
He was feeding the cat.

She went to the barber's
To buy him a wig;
But when she came back
He was dancing a jig.

She went to the cobbler's
To buy him some shoes;
But when she came back
He was reading the news.

She went to the seamstress
To buy him some linen;
But when she came back
The dog was a-spinning.

She went to the hosier's
To buy him some hose;
But when she came back
He was dressed in his clothes.

The dame made a curtsey,
The dog made a bow;
The dame said, 'Your servant,'
The dog said, 'Bow-wow.'

Two little dicky birds
Sat upon a wall,

One called Peter,
One called Paul.

Fly away Peter,
Fly away Paul;

Come back Peter,
Come back Paul.

Peter Piper picked a peck
of pickled pepper;
A peck of pickled pepper
Peter Piper picked.
If Peter Piper picked a peck
of pickled pepper,
Where's the peck of pickled pepper
Peter Piper picked?

Here we go round the mulberry bush,
The mulberry bush, the mulberry bush,
Here we go round the mulberry bush,
On a cold and frosty morning.

Little Miss Muffet
Sat on a tuffet,
Eating her curds and whey;
There came a big spider,
Who sat down beside her
And frightened Miss Muffet away.

I see the moon,
And the moon sees me;
God bless the moon,
And God bless me.

See-saw, Margery Daw,
Johnny shall have a new master;
He shall have but a penny a day,
Because he can't work any faster.

Ding, dong, bell,
Pussy's in the well.
Who put her in?
Little Johnny Green.

Who pulled her out?
Little Tommy Stout.
What a naughty boy was that
To try to drown poor pussy cat,
Who never did him any harm,
But killed the mice in his father's barn.

The Three Bears

Once upon a time in a cottage deep in the woods, lived three bears. There was Father Bear, Mother Bear and a tiny little Baby Bear.

The Bear family lived very happily inside the cottage. Each bear had its own bed, its own chair and its own bowl.

Every morning Mother Bear got up early. She made a big saucepan full of porridge on the kitchen stove. When it was cooked, she poured the porridge into three bowls and put them on the kitchen table.

There was a great big bowl for Father Bear, a middle-sized bowl for Mother Bear and a tiny bowl for Baby Bear.

First Father Bear took a big mouthful. "My porridge is too hot," he yelled in a great loud voice.

Then Mother Bear tasted a spoonful. "Oh dear!" she gasped. "This porridge is very hot indeed."

Then last of all Baby Bear sat down in front of his tiny bowl. "My porridge is too hot as well," cried Baby Bear in his squeaky voice. And he began to cry.

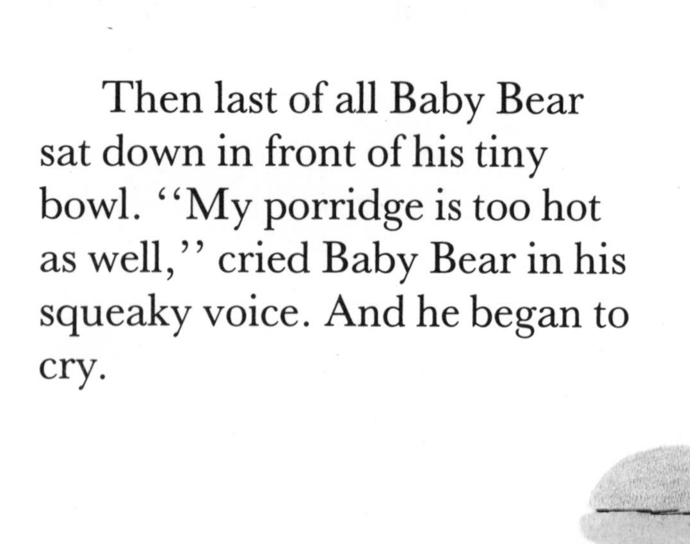

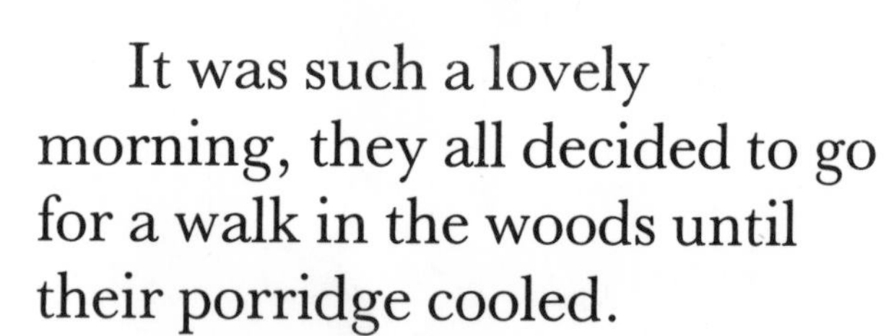

It was such a lovely morning, they all decided to go for a walk in the woods until their porridge cooled.

No sooner had they left the cottage than a little girl came skipping along the path. Her name was Goldilocks, because she had lots of golden curls. All of a sudden, through a clearing in the trees, she spied the bears' cottage.

"I wonder who lives in here?" she cried. "I think I'll take a look inside."

She peeped in the door and saw three bowls of porridge on the table, just ready to eat.

Goldilocks was so hungry she decided to try some. The first was too hot, the second too sweet, but the third little bowl was just right. Goldilocks gobbled the lot.

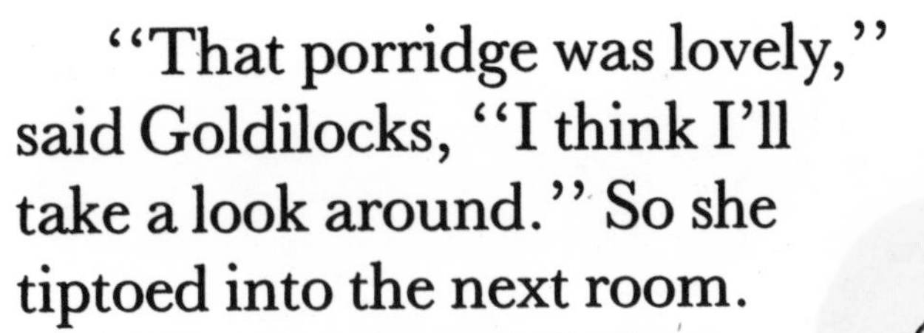

"That porridge was lovely," said Goldilocks, "I think I'll take a look around." So she tiptoed into the next room.

First she found Father Bear's great big chair — but it was too high for her to reach.

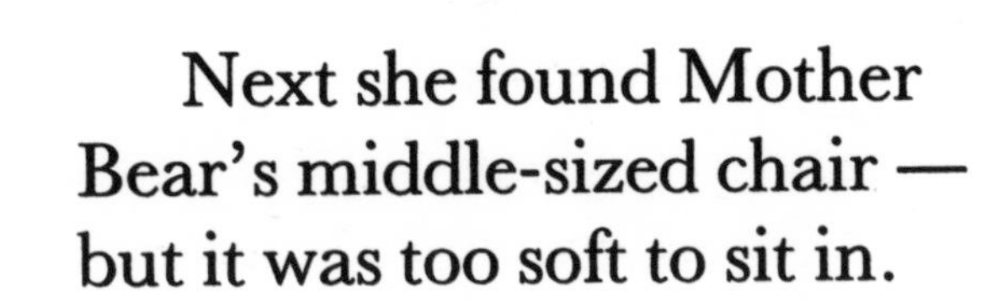

Next she found Mother Bear's middle-sized chair — but it was too soft to sit in.

Then she spotted Baby Bear's tiny chair. So she sat down. Suddenly, there was a loud CRACK, and the chair broke. Poor Goldilocks fell with a thump onto the floor.

Now Goldilocks was feeling rather sleepy, so she crept upstairs to have a little rest. First she saw Father Bear's great big bed. Goldilocks climbed up, but it was so hard and uncomfortable she soon jumped off.

Next she tried Mother Bear's middle-sized bed, but it was so soft Goldilocks sank right down into the covers. Quickly she scrambled out again.

At last she found Baby Bear's little tiny bed. It looked so comfortable, she pulled back the covers and jumped in. Very soon she was fast asleep.

But who's this walking along the path up to the cottage door? It's the three bears back from their morning walk . . . feeling very hungry!

When Father Bear saw his great big bowl, he began to shout, "Somebody has been eating my porridge!"

When Mother Bear saw her middle-sized bowl, she said in a cross voice, "Somebody has been eating my porridge!"

When Baby Bear saw his empty bowl he cried, "Somebody has been eating my porridge and has eaten it all up!"

Then Father Bear said, "Somebody has been sitting in my chair."

And Mother Bear said, "Somebody has been sitting in my chair as well."

Poor Baby Bear cried, "Somebody has been sitting in my chair and has broken it in bits."

The three bears rushed upstairs to see what they could find.

"Somebody has been sleeping in my bed," Father Bear growled.

"And somebody has been sleeping in my bed, too," Mother Bear cried.

"Somebody has been sleeping in my bed," shouted Baby Bear, "and here she is!"

All this shouting woke poor Goldilocks up. What a shock she got when she saw the three bears peering down at her.

Goldilocks jumped out of bed, ran down the stairs and out of the cottage as fast as she could. She ran down the path and all the way home. And to this day, Goldilocks has never gone walking in the woods alone.

Jack and Jill
Went up the hill,
To fetch a pail of water;

Jack fell down,
And broke his crown,
And Jill came tumbling after.

Doctor Foster went to Gloucester
In a shower of rain;
He stepped in a puddle,
Right up to his middle,
And never went there again.

Girls and boys come out to play,
The moon doth shine as bright as day.
Leave your supper and leave your sleep,
And come with your playfellows into the street.
Come with a whoop and come with a call,
Come with a good will or not at all.
Up the ladder and down the wall,
A half-penny loaf will serve us all;
You find milk, and I'll find flour,
And we'll have a pudding in half an hour.

The Man in the Moon
Looked out of the moon,
Looked out of the moon and said,
"'Tis time for all children on the earth
To think about getting to bed!"

I love little pussy,
Her coat is so warm,
And if I don't hurt her,
She'll do me no harm.
So I'll not pull her tail,
Or drive her away,
But Pussy and I
Very gently will play.
She will sit by my side,
And I'll give her some food,
And she'll like me because
I am gentle and good.

Fee, fi, fo, fum,
I smell the blood of an Englishman:
Be he alive or be he dead,
I'll grind his bones to make my bread.

Here am I,
little Jumping Joan,
When I'm by myself,
I'm all alone.

Hark, hark, the dogs do bark,
The beggars are coming to town;
Some in rags and some in jags,
And one in a velvet gown.

Ring-a-ring o'roses,
A pocket full of posies,
A-tishoo! A-tishoo!
We all fall down.

Charley Parley stole the barley
Out of the baker's shop.
The baker came out,
and gave him a clout,
Which made poor Charley hop.

There was an old woman who lived in a shoe;
She had so many children she didn't know what to do.
She gave them some broth without any bread;
Then whipped them all soundly and put them to bed.

Rock-a-bye, baby, on the tree-top.
When the wind blows
The cradle will rock;

When the bough breaks,
The cradle will fall,
Down will come baby,
Cradle and all.

Heeper-peeper, chimney sweeper,
Had a wife and couldn't keep her.
Had another, didn't love her,
Up the chimney he did shove her.

Please to remember
The fifth of November,
Gunpowder treason and plot;
I see no reason
Why gunpowder treason
Should ever be forgot.

BEAUTY AND THE BEAST

Once upon a time there lived a very rich merchant. He owned a splendid house and beautiful gardens. He had three ships which sailed to many countries and brought back lots of treasure.

The merchant had four sons and three daughters. The youngest was so lovely that everyone called her Beauty. The two elder daughters were lazy and bad-tempered, but Beauty was both kind and gentle.

One dreadful day a messenger arrived with very bad news. One of the merchant's ships had sunk, another had been attacked by pirates and the third was lost at sea.

The merchant was ruined, overnight he became a poor man. His two elder daughters stamped and screamed because they could have no more jewels or fine clothes.

However, the youngest daughter, Beauty, comforted her father. "I love you more than money or clothes," she said kindly. "Be happy! We still have each other."

Because they were now so poor, they had to move out of their splendid house and live in a tiny cottage. The sisters hated their plain clothes and humble home.

On the other hand, Beauty was never more happy. She cooked and cleaned from morning 'til night and took care of the whole family.

One day another messenger came to see the merchant. This time he brought good news. The ship everyone thought was lost, had returned full of treasure.

The merchant set out at once to bring back his fortune. But before he left he asked each of his daughters what special gift they would like him to bring back.

"As many jewels as you can find," snapped one.

"As many clothes as you can carry," sneered the other.

Beauty just smiled. "In my garden there are no flowers, only vegetables, so I would like a single red rose!"

When he came to the end of his long journey, the merchant was in for a great shock. Thieves had boarded his ship during the night and stolen all his treasure. Feeling very tired and down-hearted, the poor merchant set off for home.

For many hours along the road, his head hung down in despair. Something made him look up — there in the distance he could see a magnificent house. The merchant felt he had to take a closer look. And there growing in the middle of the garden was a beautiful red rose. "I must take it home for Beauty," said the merchant and he reached out and picked the flower.

At once the garden was filled with a terrifying sound, like the roar of an angry lion. The merchant fell on his knees in fear.

There in front of him stood a terrible beast. He had the face of a lion and the body of a man, his teeth were sharp and his claws long.

"It is death to steal my roses!" snarled the Beast. How the merchant begged the Beast to spare his life. Quickly he told the Beast all about his misfortunes, and his promise to bring Beauty back a single red rose.

"Merchant," growled the Beast. "I will spare your life on one condition. Bring one of your daughters back here to live with me — or you will die!"

The merchant was too afraid to say no so he gave his word and turned away sadly.

When he reached home, his family were overjoyed to see him, until he told them of his promise to the Beast. Then their joy soon turned to sorrow.

"You can go!" the two sisters shrieked, pointing at Beauty. "You asked for the stupid red rose — not us!" Straight away kind Beauty said: "I will go back with you father, I'm sure the Beast means no harm."

Feeling very unhappy, Beauty and her father said farewell and set off on their journey. Strange to say, the nearer they came to the Beast's home — the more beautiful the scenery became.

At last they arrived and passed through the gates into the garden. Beauty had never seen anything so lovely. Flowers bloomed and butterflies danced and peacocks strutted on the lawns. In front of the fountains a table was set full of food, in case they felt hungry after their journey.

As soon as they had eaten, without any warning, the Beast appeared! He came towards Beauty, his great shaggy head bowed low. Beauty was really afraid, but she tried not to show it.

Soon it was time for her father to return home, and Beauty was left alone with the Beast.

Inside the great house, Beauty was given her own room with everything she could ever want to make her happy. The Beast had done his best to make her feel welcome.

On the table in her room the Beast had left her a magic mirror. Whenever Beauty looked into it, she could see her home, her father and brothers and even her bad-tempered sisters.

The Beast was so kind to her, that Beauty became very fond of him.

One day, as she gazed into the magic mirror, she saw her father lying on his bed looking very ill.

She found the Beast at once and begged him to let her return home. He loved her so much that he agreed. "Return in three months or I might die," he told her. Then he gave Beauty a ring. "Put it on when you wish to return to me."

So Beauty set off for home, feeling sad to leave the Beast as well as longing to see her father.

Although the merchant was very ill, he felt much better when he saw his daughter safe and well.

So happy was Beauty at home with her family, that three months soon slipped by.

One morning, Beauty happened to glance into her magic mirror, and there was the Beast looking very ill indeed. "I must return at once," cried Beauty, "or my poor Beast will die!" Quickly she found the ring the Beast had given her.

The moment she slipped it on her finger she found herself back in the Beast's home.

Beauty ran from room to room searching for the Beast, but the house was empty. She searched everywhere in the gardens and called his name, but there was no answer.

Last of all she went to the place she loved the best — the rose garden. There lay the Beast stretched out on the grass.

"I should have come back sooner," Beauty sobbed. "I'm afraid my poor Beast is dead."

She knelt beside him and hugged him. "Don't die, dear Beast!" she begged. "You have been so kind to me that I have grown to love you."

As she spoke these words, lightning lit up the sky and the Beast became a handsome Prince.

"You have broken the spell cast on me by a wicked witch," cried the Prince. "At last I am free to ask you to marry me."

In a little while Beauty did marry the Prince and they were very happy together.

The Prince asked Beauty's father and brothers to come and live with them, but not the bad tempered sisters!

Some times Beauty and the Prince got out the magic mirror to look at them both in their cottage, still arguing and fighting with each other. And I expect they always will!

Red Riding Hood

Once upon a time there was a little girl who lived with her parents in a cottage on the edge of a forest. Her father was a woodcutter. He worked all day long in the forest, chopping down trees with his huge axe.

Right in the middle of the forest was another cottage. It belonged to the little girl's Grandmother.

The kind old lady loved her grand-daughter very much, so one day she decided to make her a present. It was a red cloak with a red hood to match.

The cloak looked so nice that the little girl wore it all the time. And that is why everybody called her Red Riding Hood.

But one day the Grandmother felt ill, so Red Riding Hood's mother baked her a cake and made her some fresh butter — just to make her feel better.

"Red Riding Hood," called her mother. "Take this cake and butter to Grandmother's cottage, a visit from you will cheer her up!"

So Red Riding Hood picked up the basket, waved goodbye to her mother and went off down the path.

She hadn't gone very far when she met a wolf. He trotted up pretending to be friendly. "Good morning, Red Riding Hood. What have you got in your basket today?"

"I have some fresh butter and cake," replied the little girl. "They are for my Grandmother, who lives in the middle of the forest. She is ill and needs cheering up."

The wolf licked his lips. "How I would love to gobble this tasty little girl up. But if I am clever, I can eat her Grandmother as well," he sniggered. "Red Riding Hood," said the wolf slyly. "We will both go to visit your Grandmother and cheer her up. I'll race you there!"

Then the clever wolf said to Red Riding Hood, "You follow this path and I will find another one. Then we'll see who reaches Grandmother's cottage first."

No sooner was Red Riding Hood out of sight than the wolf ran off at top speed.

As for Red Riding Hood, she wandered slowly along the path picking flowers and wild strawberries for her Grandmother. She had forgotten all about the race.

That wicked wolf knew every secret path and short cut in the forest. He ran so fast, the animals and birds never even noticed him.

Quietly he crept round a clearing in the trees where the woodcutter was chopping wood. On and on he raced until he came to the middle of the forest.

The wolf reached Grandmother's cottage in next to no time. He ran up the path and knocked on the door.

"Who is that?" cried Grandmother from her bed. "It is Red Riding Hood," replied the wolf in his softest voice. "Lift the latch and come right in," the old lady called, "the door isn't locked, my dear."

The wolf bounded in and swallowed poor Grandmother in one bite!

“That was delicious,” sighed the wicked wolf, smacking his lips. “Now for Red Riding Hood!”

The wolf looked round the bedroom. He found one of Grandmother's spare nightdresses and her nightcap, so he put them on as fast as he could.

Then he noticed a spare pair of Grandmother's glasses, so he stuck them on the end of his nose. Then the wolf jumped into bed and waited for Red Riding Hood.

At last the little girl reached the cottage door and tapped very gently. "Who is it?" asked the wolf (trying to sound like Grandmother).

"It's Red Riding Hood and I've brought you some cake and fresh butter."

The wolf grinned. "Lift the latch and walk right in," he croaked.

So Red Riding Hood opened the door and came inside. "You sound very strange," called Red Riding Hood up the stairs to her Grandmother. "I have a cold, my dear!" the wolf replied. "Come upstairs so that I can see you."

Little Red Riding Hood was rather shocked when she saw her Grandmother. She looked so different.

"Why, Grandmother, what strong arms you have!" said the little girl.

"All the better to hug you with!" replied the wolf.

"Why, Grandmother, what big ears you have!" said Red Riding Hood.

"All the better to hear you with!" the wolf cried.

"Why, Grandmother, what big eyes you have!" said Red Riding Hood staring at him.

"All the better to see you with!" the wolf grinned.

"Why, Grandmother, what big teeth you have!" gasped Red Riding Hood.

"All the better to EAT you with!" snarled the wolf. And he threw back the bed clothes and leapt out of bed.

Poor Red Riding Hood screamed at the top of her voice, as the wolf tried to grab her and gobble her up. She escaped from the bedroom and dashed down the stairs — the hungry wolf close behind!

Now, Red Riding Hood's father was chopping wood nearby and he heard the little girl's screams.

The woodcutter grabbed his huge axe and ran towards the cottage. he saw the wolf chasing Red Riding Hood and guessed what had happened. The brave woodcutter raised his axe and chopped the wolf in two with one blow. The wolf fell dead, and Red Riding Hood was saved.

The frightened little girl ran to her father and kissed and hugged him.

But what a surprise they got when they turned round . . . there stood Grandmother safe and sound! Because the woodcutter had chopped the wolf in two, Grandmother was able to climb out quite unharmed.

So all three went back inside the cottage. They unpacked the basket Red Riding Hood had brought and had some cake spread with fresh butter.

Little Red Riding Hood never again went walking in the forest alone. And Grandmother took great care to lock her cottage door.

Polly put the kettle on,
Polly put the kettle on,
Polly put the kettle on,
We'll all have tea.

Sukey take it off again,
Sukey take it off again,
Sukey take it off again,
They've all gone away.

It's raining, it's pouring,
The old man's snoring;
He got into bed
And bumped his head
And couldn't get up in the morning.

Old Mother Goose,
When she wanted to wander,
Would ride through the air
On a very fine gander.

Mother Goose had a house,
'Twas built in a wood,
Where an owl at the door
For sentinel stood.

Hickory, dickory, dock,
The mouse ran up the clock.
The clock struck one,
The mouse ran down,
Hickory, dickory, dock.

Jack be nimble,
Jack be quick,
Jack jump over
The candlestick.

As I was going to St Ives,
I met a man with seven wives;

Each wife had seven sacks,

Each sack had seven cats,

Each cat had seven kits:

Kits, cats, sacks and wives
How many were going to St Ives?

Little Blue Ben, who lives in the glen,
Keeps a blue cat and one blue hen,
Which lays of blue eggs a score and ten;
Where shall I find the little Blue Ben?

Yankee Doodle came to town,
Riding on a pony,
He stuck a feather in his cap
And called it macaroni.

Bobby Shaftoe's gone to sea,
Silver buckles on his knee;
He'll come back and marry me,
Bonny Bobby Shaftoe.

Bobby Shaftoe's bright and fair,
Combing down his yellow hair,
He's my love for evermore,
Bonny Bobby Shaftoe.

This little pig went to market;

This little pig stayed at home;

This little pig had roast beef;

This little pig had none;
And this little pig cried, Wee-wee-wee!
All the way home.

Thirty days hath September,
April, June and November;
All the rest have thirty-one.
Excepting February alone,
And that has twenty-eight days clear
And twenty-nine in each leap year.

Rub-a-dub-dub,
Three men in a tub,
And how do you think they got there?
The butcher, the baker,
The candlestick-maker,
They all jumped out of a rotten potato.
'Twas enough to make a fish stare.

Humpty Dumpty sat on a wall,
Humpty Dumpty had a great fall;
All the King's horses,
And all the King's men,
Couldn't put Humpty together again.

A diller, a dollar,
A ten o'clock scholar,
What makes you come so soon?
You used to come at ten o'clock,
But now you come at noon.

Pat-a-cake, pat-a-cake, baker's man,
Bake me a cake as fast as you can;
Pat it and prick it, and mark it with B,
Put it in the oven for Baby and me.

Aladdin

This strange story happened in a city in far-off China many years ago. It is a tale of a magic lamp, a magic ring, an evil magician and many more amazing things. But most of all, it is a story about a boy called Aladdin.

Aladdin was the son of a poor widow. Although his mother worked hard to earn a little money, her son did nothing to help her. He spent all his time with his friends, day-dreaming of becoming a rich man.

One day, as Aladdin was just lazing around, a stranger came up to him. "I am your uncle from Africa," said the man. "Go home and tell your mother I am coming to visit her."

For once Aladdin did as he was told.

The poor widow used all the money she had to buy food for the stranger's supper. After he had eaten, the man promised to make them both rich. Aladdin was delighted — but his mother was not so sure.

"All I ask," said the stranger, "is that Aladdin do one small task for me tomorrow in return."

Now as you may have guessed, the stranger was not Aladdin's uncle at all. He was really a powerful magician in disguise. He was not out to help Aladdin — but trick him.

Very early next morning, Aladdin and the magician left the city. By the time it was light they had reached the mountains. As they climbed up and up, the path grew narrower with steep rocks on each side. At long last they stopped. They could go no further for a huge boulder blocked their path.

Aladdin sat down to rest, but not for long! The magician pointed a long finger at the boulder and shouted, "Abracadabra". A noise like thunder echoed round the mountains, the boulder vanished, and the rock behind cracked in two.

The magician grabbed hold of Aladdin. "Go through that crack in the rock, because I am too big. You will find some steps which lead to a cave, in the cave you will see an old lamp. Bring it to me straight away."

Poor Aladdin tried to run away, but the evil magician held him too tightly.

"If you are such a coward," bellowed the magician, "take my magic ring." And with that he pushed Aladdin through the crack in the rock, and the poor boy fell down the steps and into the cave.

When Aladdin picked himself up, he could hardly believe his eyes. The cave was full of gold and jewels. Aladdin gasped. He picked up a few and stuffed them in his pocket to take back to his mother.

Outside the cave the magician began to shout, "Bring me my lamp at once!" But Aladdin was too busy to hear him.

Because Aladdin did not obey him at once, the magician flew into a terrible rage. He shouted the magic word "Abracadabra" and the crack in the rock closed and Aladdin was trapped.

The poor boy buried his head in his hands in despair. Now quite by chance he rubbed the magic ring on his finger. Immediately the cave was filled with a loud swishing noise, and an enormous genie appeared. "I'm the Genie of the Ring, O Master! Speak, and I obey!"

"Take me home," gasped Aladdin.

"Your wish is my command," answered the genie. "But first, O Master, take this old lamp. Inside is a genie more powerful than me, and you will become his master."

A great roaring sound filled the air, and Aladdin found himself being carried back home by a genie twice as large as the first one.

Aladdin's mother screamed with fright, until he told her of his adventures and the wonderful lamp.

At last Aladdin's dream had come true and they were no longer poor. He soon became the richest man in the land, thanks to the Genie of the Lamp. The Emperor became his friend and invited him to his court.

One day Aladdin met the Emperor's daughter, and he fell in love with her at once. Aladdin dare not ask the Emperor if he could marry the Princess. So he rubbed the lamp and asked the genie to fill the whole of the Emperor's garden with treasure.

Then the Emperor gladly gave his consent. Aladdin rubbed his lamp again, and a beautiful new palace appeared for Aladdin and the Princess to live in.

Far away in Africa, the evil magician heard about Aladdin's palace. He guessed at once that Aladdin had the lamp.

Straight away he travelled to China. He disguised himself as an old lamp-seller and waited by the gates of Aladdin's palace. "New lamps for old," he cried loudly. He didn't have to wait long before a servant brought out all the old lamps from the palace.

The evil magician saw his lamp and grabbed it with glee. He ordered the genie to take him, the palace and the Princess back to his home in Africa.

When Aladdin returned home he could find no trace of his Princess or his palace.

As he sat wondering what to do, quite by accident he rubbed the magic ring. At once the genie appeared. "Take me to my Princess, O Genie of the Ring!" Aladdin begged.

Before he could even blink, he found himself standing outside her bedroom window. The Princess was overjoyed to see Aladdin. "I know where the lamp is," she whispered. "The magician keeps it tied to his belt night and day."

Quickly Aladdin told her his plan.

"Take this sleeping powder and mix it in his wine. You must steal the lamp as soon as he falls asleep!"

Late that night the Princess dropped the powder into the Magician's glass, although she was very frightened. He fell asleep at once and she carefully untied the lamp.

Aladdin jumped out from his hiding place and grabbed the lamp. One rub and the genie appeared. "Take us all home!" Aladdin cried.

The genie's magic was so powerful, he was able to whisk the palace, the Princess, Aladdin and all the servants back home to China.

"Drop that evil magician into the sea on the way home!" ordered Aladdin.

The Emperor and Aladdin's mother were waiting to welcome them all back home. At last their adventures were over.

As for the lamp, Aladdin made sure it was kept in a very safe place — and never given away again.

Three little kittens
They lost their mittens,
And they began to cry,
Oh, Mother dear,
We sadly fear
Our mittens we have lost.
What! Lost your mittens,
You naughty kittens!
Then you shall have no pie.
Mee-ow, mee-ow, mee-ow.
No, you shall have no pie.

The three little kittens
They found their mittens,
And they began to cry,
Oh, Mother dear,
See here, see here,
Our mittens we have found.
Put on your mittens,
You silly kittens,
And you shall have some pie.
Purr-r, purr-r, purr-r,
Oh, let us have some pie.

The three little kittens
Put on their mittens,
And soon ate up the pie;
Oh, Mother dear,
We greatly fear
Our mittens we have soiled.
What! Soiled your mittens,
You naughty kittens!
Then they began to sigh,
Mee-ow, mee-ow, mee-ow,
Then they began to sigh.

The three little kittens
They washed their mittens,
And hung them out to dry;
Oh, Mother dear,
Do you not hear,
Our mittens we have washed.
What! Washed your mittens,
You good little kittens,
But I smell a rat close by.
Mee-ow, mee-ow, mee-ow,
We smell a rat close by.

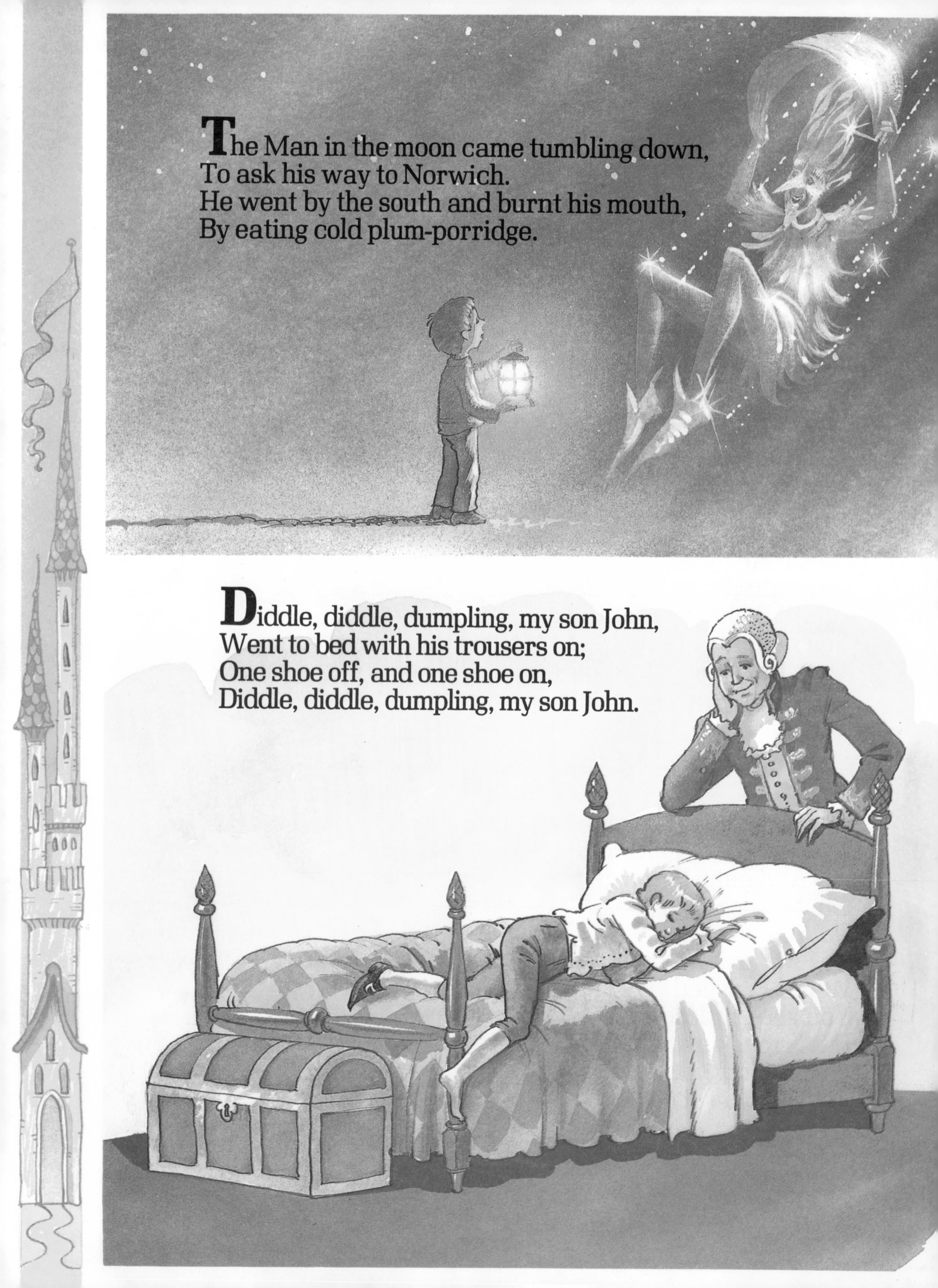

The Man in the moon came tumbling down,
To ask his way to Norwich.
He went by the south and burnt his mouth,
By eating cold plum-porridge.

Diddle, diddle, dumpling, my son John,
Went to bed with his trousers on;
One shoe off, and one shoe on,
Diddle, diddle, dumpling, my son John.

One misty, moisty morning,
When cloudy was the weather,
There I met an old man
Clothed all in leather.

I took him by the hand,
And told him very plain,
'How do you do? How do you do?
And how do you do again?'

Little Tommy Tittlemouse
Lived in a little house;
He caught fishes
In other men's ditches.

Sing a song of sixpence,
A pocket full of rye;
Four-and-twenty blackbirds,
Baked in a pie.

When the pie was opened,
The birds began to sing;
Was not that a dainty dish,
To set before the king?

The king was in his counting-house,
Counting out his money;
The queen was in the parlour
Eating bread and honey.

The maid was in the garden,
Hanging out the clothes,
When down came a blackbird
And pecked off her nose.

Little Boy Blue,
Come blow your horn.
The sheep's in the meadow,
The cow's in the corn.
Where is the boy
Who looks after the sheep?
He's under a haystack
Fast asleep.
Will you wake him?
No, not I,
For if I do,
He's sure to cry.

Pease porridge hot,
Pease porridge cold,
Pease porridge in the pot,
Nine days old.

Some like it hot, Some like it cold, Some like it in the pot,
Nine days old.

Curly Locks, Curly Locks,
Wilt thou be mine?
Thou shalt not wash dishes,
Nor yet feed the swine;

But sit on a cushion,
And sew a fine seam
And feed upon strawberries,
Sugar and cream.

SLEEPING BEAUTY

A long time ago in a kingdom far away, a baby Princess was born. The King and Queen were so happy and proud of their little daughter, they invited the most important fairies in the land to come to her christening.

The invitations were sent out and the fairies set off for the palace.

When the christening was over all the fairies crowded round the baby's cradle, the time had come for them to give the Princess her gifts.

The first fairy gave her beauty, the second gave her goodness, the third fairy said she would be charming, the fourth promised she would be clever, the fifth fairy gave her grace and the sixth fairy said she would always be happy.

All of a sudden, the door to the banqueting hall burst open. Standing there was the ugliest most evil-looking fairy you can imagine!

"Why was I not invited?" she screamed.

The evil fairy shook with anger as she went up to the cradle. The King and Queen trembled as she pointed at the baby Princess.

"Before she is sixteen, the Princess will prick her finger on a spindle and die!" And with a terrible cackle of laughter, she vanished.

Everyone was shocked by the wicked fairy's spell, and the poor Queen began to cry.

Just at that moment the smallest fairy stepped from behind a pillar where she had been hiding.

"I have not yet given the Princess my gift," she said in a kind voice. "The Princess will not die — but fall asleep for one hundred years. Then a young Prince will come and wake her with a kiss, and the evil spell will be broken."

That very day the King sent out messengers all over the land.

All the spindles and the spinning wheels were smashed or burned. He made a very strict law that no-one should ever use a spindle again. This way the King hoped to save his dear Princess from the fairy's evil spell.

Sixteen years past. The Princess grew up beautiful, good, charming and happy, in fact she grew up with all the gifts the fairies had promised.

One day she was gazing up at the palace, when she noticed an open window at the very top of the highest tower.

"I wonder if anyone lives up there?" said the Princess. "I think I'll climb right up to the top and see."

Now the palace was a wonderful place to explore, because it was so big and rambling. So the Princess climbed up the winding staircase until she found herself in front of a small door. Gently she pushed it open.

There, in a tiny attic room, sat a little old lady spinning. (She had never heard the King's very strict law about spindles — as she never left her attic room.) "What are you doing?" asked the Princess, very interested.

"Just spinning wool, my dear!" smiled the old lady.

"May I try?" asked the Princess, and she reached out for the spindle. As she touched the sharp point, it pricked her finger.

The evil fairy's spell had worked. At once the Princess fell to the floor in a deep sleep.

When the King and Queen were told what had happened, and when they saw the Princess asleep, they knew the evil spell had come true. Their beloved daughter would sleep for a hundred years.

The servants carried the Princess from the attic room and laid her on a beautiful velvet-covered bed.

Now the good fairy (who promised the Princess would not die) came at once to the Palace. Without a word she touched everybody with her wand.

She touched the cooks in the kitchen, and the servants who waited at the Palace banqueting table.

She touched the guards and the footmen, the pages and the maids.

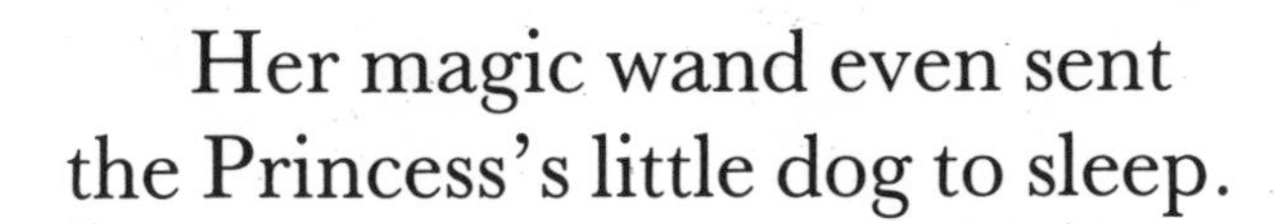

Her magic wand even sent the Princess's little dog to sleep.

A strange silence fell over everything. Gently, her wand touched the King and Queen before she flew away from the Palace.

The good fairy waved her wand for the last time and a thick forest sprang up around the Palace. Tangled briar and thorns crept over the paths and up the walls. This way no-one could cut through the undergrowth or visit the sleeping Palace, until one hundred years had gone by.

As time passed people forgot all about the Palace and the sleeping Princess.

One day a handsome Prince was out hunting nearby. He happened to look up and saw the very tops of the Palace towers peeping above the trees.

From out of nowhere the good fairy appeared! She told him of the Princess and the evil spell that only a handsome Prince like him could break.

At once the Prince drew his sword and began to cut a path through the thick brambles.

Very soon he reached the Palace. He passed snoring guards and sleeping ladies and gentlemen.

The Palace cat was snoozing peacefully on a cushion.

There were even a couple of mice fast asleep under the table in the banqueting hall.

They had all been asleep for one hundred years.

Suddenly, the Prince looked up and saw the beautiful Princess asleep in her velvet-covered bed. He knelt beside her and kissed her hand. At last the evil spell was broken . . .

. . . And everyone woke up, just as the good fairy had planned!

The Prince and Princess fell in love and after a while they were married, and of course lived happily ever after.

To bed, to bed,
Says Sleepy-head;
Tarry a while, says Slow;
Put on the pan,
Says Greedy Nan,
We'll sup before we go.

See a pin and pick it up,
All the day you'll have good luck.
See a pin and let it lay,
Bad luck you'll have all the day.

Peter, Peter, pumpkin eater,
Had a wife and couldn't keep her;
He put her in a pumpkin shell,
And there he kept her very well.

If I had a donkey that wouldn't go,
Would I beat him? Oh no, no.
I'd put him in the barn and give him some corn.
The best little donkey that ever was born.

Jingle, bells! Jingle, bells!
Jingle all the way;
Oh, what fun it is to ride
In a one-horse open sleigh.

Hot cross buns! Hot cross buns!
One a penny, two a penny,
Hot cross buns!
If you have no daughters
Give them to your sons;
One a penny, two a penny
Hot cross buns.

To market, to market, to buy a fat pig,
Home again, home again, jiggety-jig;

Pussy cat, pussy cat,
Where have you been?
I've been to London
To look at the Queen.

Pussy cat, pussy cat,
What did you there?
I frightened a little mouse
Under her chair.

To market, to market, to buy a fat hog,
Home again, home again, jiggety-jog.

Baa, baa, black sheep,
Have you any wool?
Yes, sir, yes, sir,
Three bags full;

One for the master,
And one for the dame,
And one for the little boy
Who lives down the lane.

Little Jack Horner
Sat in the corner,
Eating his Christmas pie;
He put in his thumb,
And pulled out a plum,
And said, What a good boy am I!

'Oranges and lemons,'
Say the bells of St Clement's.

'You owe me five farthings,'
Say the bells of St Martin's.

'When will you pay me?'
Say the bells of Old Bailey.

'When I grow rich,'
Say the bells of Shoreditch.

'When will that be?'
Say the bells of Stepney.

'I'm sure I don't know,'
Says the Great Bell of Bow.

Here comes the candle
To light you to bed,
Here comes the chopper,
To chop off your head.

One, two, three, four, five,
Once I caught a fish alive,
Six, seven, eight, nine, ten,
Then I let it go again.

Why did you let it go?
Because it bit my finger so.
Which finger did it bite?
This little finger on the right.

Three blind mice, see how they run!
They all ran after the farmer's wife,
Who cut off their tails with a carving knife,
Did you ever see such a thing in your life,
As three blind mice?

Mary had a little lamb,
Its fleece was white as snow;
And everywhere that Mary went
The lamb was sure to go.

It followed her to school one day,
That was against the rule;
It made the children laugh and play
To see a lamb at school.

Cobbler, cobbler mend my shoe,
Get it done by half past two,
Stitch it up and stitch it down
And then I'll give you half a crown.

There was a little girl
Who had a little curl
Right in the middle of her forehead.

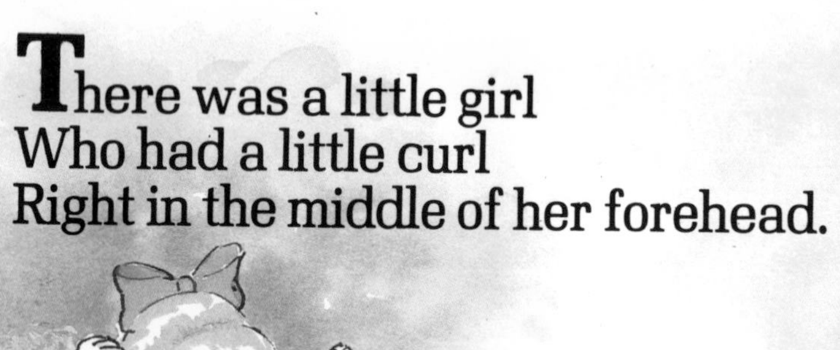

When she was good,
She was very, very good;
But when she was bad, she was horrid.

The Gingerbread Man

Once upon a time there lived an old woman, an old man and a little boy. Now one day the old woman was so busy in her kitchen she asked the little boy to help her. They were going to do some baking while the old man went into the garden to dig.

"Let's get started," said the old woman. "We have lots to do today." She told the little boy that if he worked hard, he could make something special.

The little boy found the rolling pin and baking tins. Next he got out the flour, the eggs and the butter. He weighed the sugar and beat the eggs. He even rolled out the pastry.

Very soon they had baked a big pile of cakes and pies. They made fancy little cakes with icing and sweets on top, and buns covered in chocolate and tarts filled with red jam. They looked delicious.

‘‘We’re almost done,’’ said the old woman with a smile. ‘‘Have a look in my cookery book and find something special you would like to bake.’’

The little boy opened the book and found it at once. ‘‘I want to make the biggest Gingerbread Man in the world,’’ he cried.

So the little boy found the largest baking tin that would fit into the oven. He cut out the Gingerbread Man shape then he gave him currants for eyes and buttons, and a slice of lemon peel for a mouth.

The old woman put the Gingerbread Man into the oven, and told the boy to keep an eye on him, while she went out into the garden.

It wasn't very long before he heard strange noises coming from the oven. First a tapping, then a banging and then a very loud knocking.

All at once, the oven door burst open, and out jumped the Gingerbread Man.

He dashed past the little boy and straight out the kitchen door. He ran outside, down the path, and out of the garden gate.

The old man, the old woman and the little boy began to chase after him. But the Gingerbread Man laughed and shouted, "Run! Run! As fast as you can! You can't catch me, I'm the Gingerbread Man!"

"Free at last," he shouted, as he ran over hills and away. "No-one can catch me and eat me up — because I'm the Gingerbread Man."

On his way he passed some men resting under a tree. "Can't catch me," yelled the Gingerbread Man, as he sped by.

"It's too hot to run," shouted the men, "but if you come any closer, we'll eat you for our dinner."

But the Gingerbread Man just stuck out his tongue.

By now the Gingerbread Man was beginning to enjoy his freedom. He spied a big black cat fast asleep in the sun. The Gingerbread Man pulled her whiskers as he ran by.

The cat sprang up and chased after the Gingerbread Man trying to catch him with her sharp claws. "Run! Run! As fast as you can! You can't catch me, I'm the Gingerbread Man!"

The cat ran after the Gingerbread Man for miles, but she never caught him.

On and on he ran until he heard a fierce dog barking in a garden. "Can't catch me," teased the Gingerbread Man.

The dog was so startled he jumped over the gate and ran after the Gingerbread Man. He snapped and snarled at him, and tried to bite him in half with his sharp teeth.

"Run! Run! As fast as you can! You can't catch me, I'm the Gingerbread Man!" The dog chased after him until he was too tired to go any further. But he never did catch the Gingerbread Man.

Next he passed a field of cows quietly munching the grass. The Gingerbread Man climbed up on the fence and shouted at the top of his voice. "Can't catch me, I'm the Gingerbread Man."

One of the cows lifted up her head, "I don't need to run after you," she mooed. "I can reach you from here." She was so big she almost swallowed the Gingerbread Man in one bite.

The Gingerbread Man fell off the fence in fright. He picked himself up and cried, "Run! Run! As fast as you can! You can't catch me, I'm the Gingerbread Man!" The cow went on quietly munching the grass.

The Gingerbread Man just kept on running until he came to a river. He sat down on the bank quite out of breath and feeling rather pleased with himself. "It must be true," he said out loud. "No-one can catch me. An old woman, an old man and a little boy can't catch me. The men resting under the tree couldn't either, nor could the black cat or the fierce dog, not even that silly cow."

The Gingerbread Man grinned. "I really am the most wonderful Gingerbread Man in the world."

Now hiding in the grass near the river bank was a Fox. He heard every word that the Gingerbread Man said and he licked his lips.

"Good day. What a fine looking fellow you are," called the Fox, as he strolled along the river bank towards the Gingerbread Man.

"Thank you, kind sir," smiled the Gingerbread Man. "Run! Run! As fast as you can!

You can't catch me, I'm the Gingerbread Man!''

"I wouldn't dream of trying," said the Fox slyly. "Tell me, Gingerbread Man. How are you going to cross the river? Can you swim?"

The Gingerbread Man looked rather dismayed. "I can jump. I can do hand-stands. I can even balance on one leg. However, you are quite right, Mr. Fox, I cannot swim."

"Now I can swim very well," sniggered the Fox. "I have a wonderful idea, Gingerbread Man. If you

balance on my tail, I will take you across the river."
So the Fox and the Gingerbread Man started to cross the water.

They hadn't gone very far before the Fox's tail began to get wet. "Stand on my back," said the

Fox, "and you'll be alright."

So the Gingerbread man climbed onto his back.

Deeper and deeper they went. Soon the Fox's back was under water. "Climb up onto my head," called the Fox, "or you'll get wet."

So the Gingerbread Man climbed onto his head.
A little further across the river the Fox's head began to sink under the water. "Climb up on my nose," shouted the Fox, "or you will drown."

The Gingerbread Man climbed up onto the very top of the Fox's nose.

The Fox opened his mouth wide and, SNAP, he gobbled him up in one bite.

So that was the end of the poor Gingerbread Man.

"Run! Run! As fast as you can! You can't catch me, I'm the Gingerbread Man!"

And no-one ever did catch him . . . except the Fox.